TEN *Thank-You* LETTERS

DANIEL KIRK

Nancy Paulsen Books ❂ An Imprint of Penguin Group (USA)

for Aiden

NANCY PAULSEN BOOKS
Published by the Penguin Group
Penguin Group (USA) LLC
375 Hudson Street
New York, NY 10014

USA | Canada | UK | Ireland | Australia
New Zealand | India | South Africa | China
penguin.com
A Penguin Random House Company

Library of Congress Cataloging-in-Publication Data
Kirk, Daniel. Ten thank-you letters / Daniel Kirk. pages cm
Summary: While Pig is trying to finish a thank-you note to his grandmother,
his best friend Rabbit repeatedly interrupts to borrow supplies for a series
of his own notes, thanking all of the special people in their lives.
[1. Thank-you notes—Fiction. 2. Gratitude—Fiction. 3. Best friends—Fiction.
4. Friendship—Fiction.] I. Title.
PZ7.K6339Tek 2014 [E]—dc23 2013046403

Manufactured in China by South China Printing Co. Ltd.
ISBN 978-0-399-16937-3
1 3 5 7 9 10 8 6 4 2

Design by Annie Ericsson. Title hand lettering by Annie Ericsson.
Text set in Century Schoolbook Penguin Infant and Tyke ITC Std.
The illustrations in this book were made by scanning ink-on-paper drawings and
painted plywood panels into the computer and adding textures and colors in Photoshop.

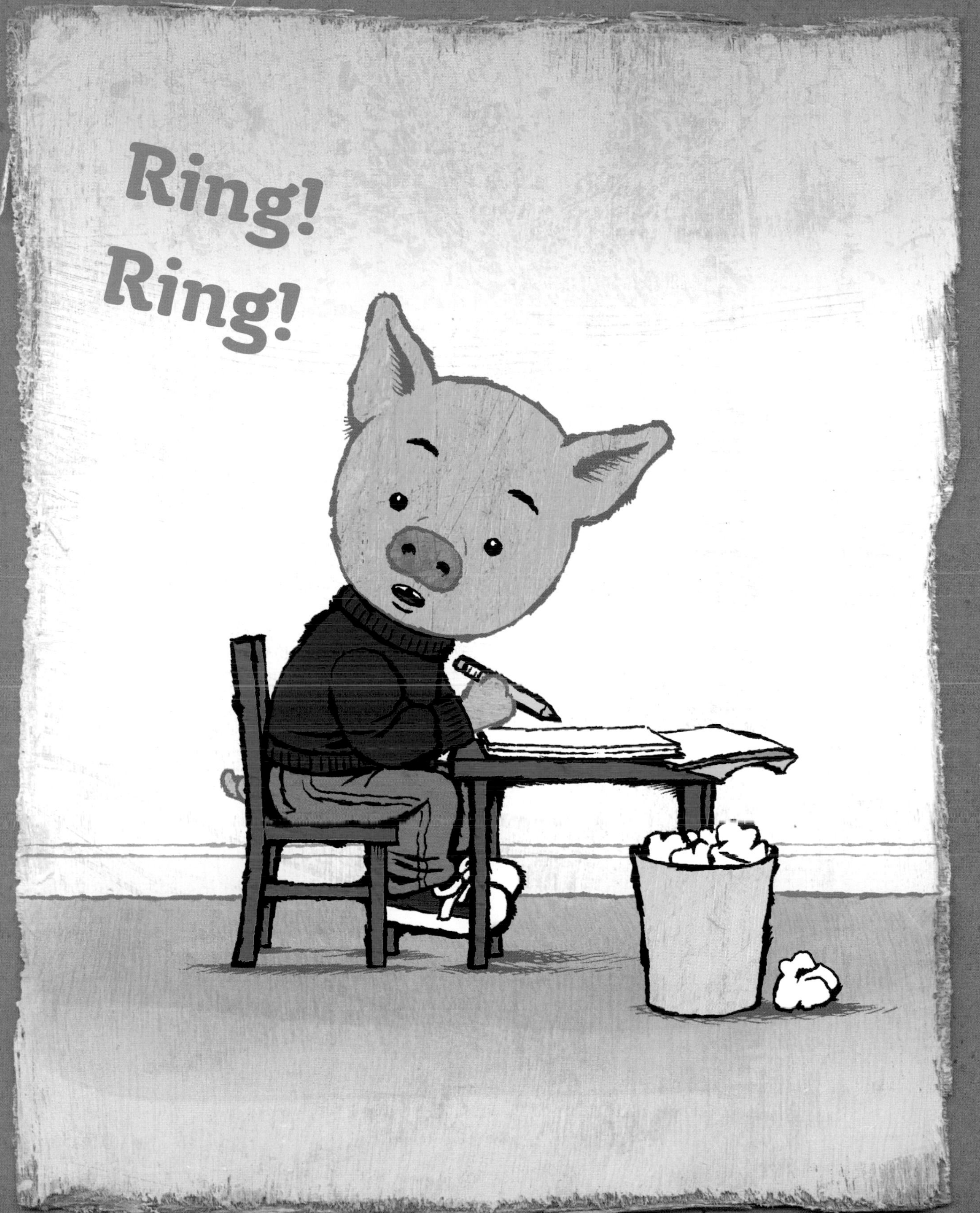
Ring!
Ring!

Hey, I just thought of another
great person to thank.
Can I borrow more paper?

Aren't you done with your letter yet, Pig?

No, Rabbit.
I just want to tell
Grandma that
I laughed so much
yesterday my loose
tooth came out!

Sorry, Pig! Maybe if you just
give me a stack of paper
and envelopes and more stamps,
I won't have to bother you!

Finally, I can finish my letter . . . Yay, done!

But . . . Rabbit used all my envelopes! And all of the stamps!

Ring! Ring!

Hello, Pig. Guess what? I got more envelopes and stamps for you.

And I wrote one more
thank-you letter.
I thought I'd deliver
it myself. Here!

Thanks, Rabbit!
No one ever wrote me
a thank-you letter before!

Dear Pig,
Thank You for
inspiring me.
And for being
generous. And
for being my friend!
Love,
Rabbit
P.S. Now are you ready
to play catch?

Yay! Game time!

Yes—after a quick stop
at the mailbox!

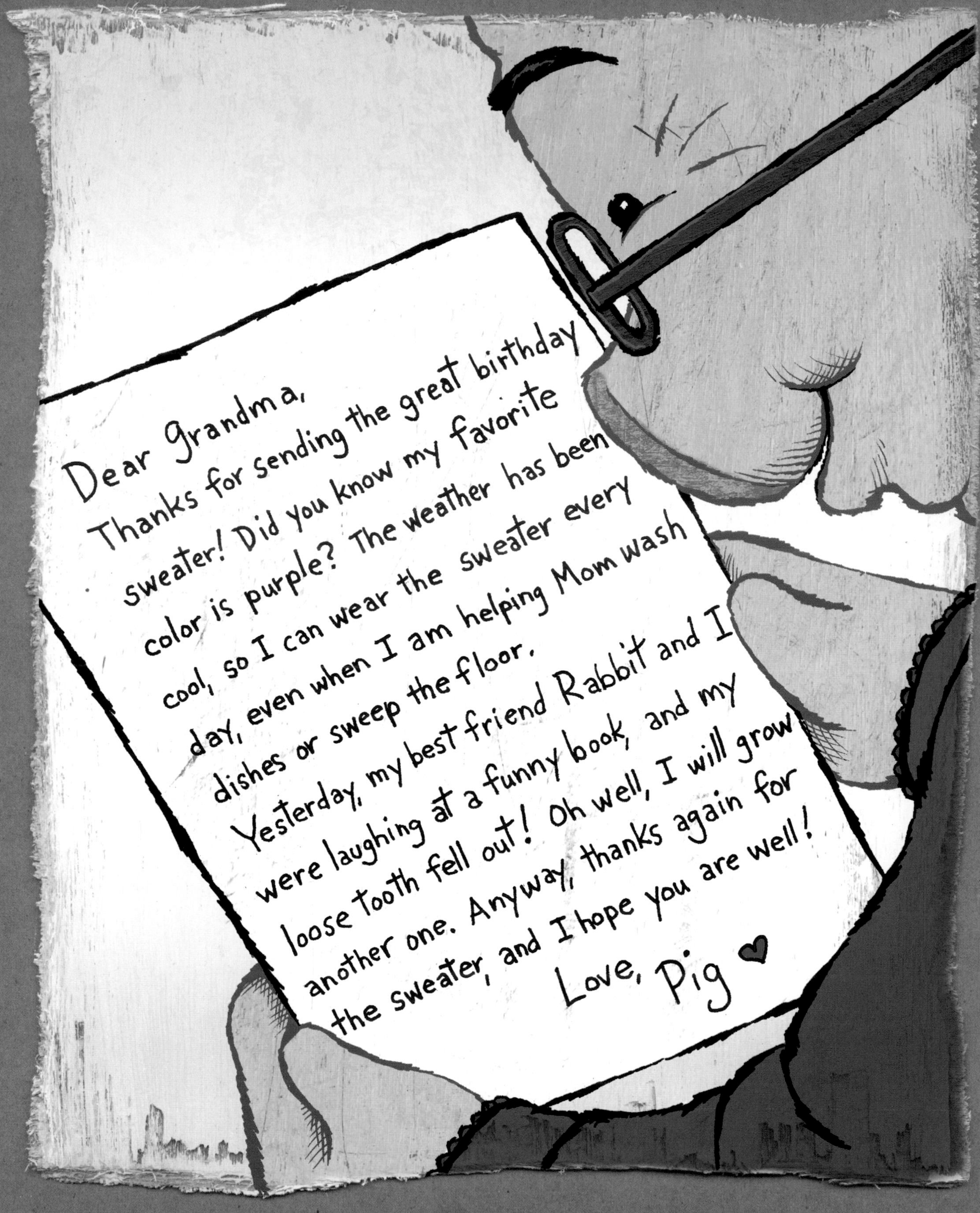
Dear Grandma,
Thanks for sending the great birthday
sweater! Did you know my favorite
color is purple? The weather has been
cool, so I can wear the sweater every
day, even when I am helping Mom wash
dishes or sweep the floor.
Yesterday, my best friend Rabbit and I
were laughing at a funny book, and my
loose tooth fell out! Oh well, I will grow
another one. Anyway, thanks again for
the sweater, and I hope you are well!
Love, Pig